Karen's Pumpkin Patch

Look for these
and other books about Karen
in the
Baby-sitters Little Sister series:

Little Sister

Karen's Pumpkin Patch

Ann M. Martin

Illustrations by Susan Tang

A
LITTLE APPLE
PAPERBACK

SCHOLASTIC INC.
New York Toronto London Auckland Sydney

This book is for
Jerry and Randi Tisch,
who would take very good care
of a pumpkin patch.

ISBN 0-590-45647-4

12 11 10 9   7/9

Printed in the U.S.A.   40

First Scholastic printing, October 1992

Spook Night

"Look at this!" cried David Michael. He held up a hunk of black hair. "Your witch wig, Karen. Remember?"

"Yup," I said. "And here is a clown mask."

"Funny!" said Emily Michelle. (Emily is two and a half. She does not talk much yet. But someday she will.)

"Here is a gross green monster hand," said Andrew.

Andrew is my brother. David Michael is my stepbrother. And Emily is my adopted sister. We were looking through a box of dress-up clothes in the playroom at Daddy's house. It was full of old Halloween costumes.

I am Karen Brewer. I am seven years old. I have blonde hair and freckles and glasses. I am in second grade at Stoneybrook Academy here in Stoneybrook, Connecticut. My teacher is Ms. Colman. I love her. Also, I love Halloween and every other holiday. Halloween would not come for awhile, but my sister and brothers and I wanted to be ready anyway.

"Are you going to be a witch again, Karen?" asked David Michael.

"Yup." I am almost always a witch. I like to read about witches — but meeting a witch in person would be scary. And guess what. I think my next-door neighbor is a witch. I cannot be sure, though.

"What are you going to be this year?" David Michael asked Andrew.

Andrew frowned. "I don't know yet. Maybe a monster. I like this monster hand.

I could get fangs and warts and make my face green."

Emily laughed. "Funny!" she said again.

"No, Emily. A monster is scary," I explained patiently.

"Scary," Emily repeated. But she was still laughing.

"I think we should all be in the Halloween parade," said David Michael.

"At the party?" I asked.

David Michael nodded. "There is going to be a haunted house, too," he added.

"Cool!" I exclaimed.

This year Halloween was going to be on a Saturday. And for the first time ever, Stoneybrook was going to have a big party downtown. Anybody could come. If you wore a costume you could walk in the parade. You could play games and bob for apples and eat candy and go through a spooky haunted house. Also, you could enter one of the pumpkin contests. There were going to be contests for pumpkins and contests for carved jack-o'-lanterns. The

4

pumpkins would win prizes for biggest or prettiest or most strangely shaped. The jack-o'-lanterns would win prizes for fanciest or scariest or funniest. I wondered what the prizes would be.

"I cannot wait for Halloween," said Andrew.

"For candy and parades and fun," said David Michael.

"For the spookiest night of the year," I added.

Emily Michelle had stopped paying attention to us. She was looking in the box of clothes again. She had picked out a tutu and a crown.

"Hey, you could be a ballerina, Emily," said Andrew.

"Nah," I replied. "That is much too ordinary. Anybody could be a ballerina. Emily, I will make you something different. How about an elf? Or a pumpkin? Or a snowflake?"

Emily had taken off the crown. She had put on a football helmet. She grinned at us.

"Emily, you can*not* be a football player!" I exclaimed.

"Why not?" asked David Michael.

"Just because."

Andrew interrupted our discussion. "Karen?" he said. "I have an idea. Maybe this year we can trick-or-treat *two* times on spook night."

Right away I knew what he meant. And it was an extra good idea. Maybe we could trick-or-treat once in Mommy's neighborhood and once in Daddy's neighborhood. We would get so, so much candy!

2

Mommies and Daddies

Not just anybody can go trick-or-treating two times. But if you are a two-two like Andrew and me, maybe you can. What is a two-two? A two-two is someone with two families. And Andrew and I have two families now. Once, we had just one family — Mommy, Daddy, Andrew, and me. We lived in Daddy's big house, the one with the box full of Halloween costumes. That is the house Daddy grew up in.

But after Mommy and Daddy had been married for awhile, they decided they did not love each other anymore. They loved Andrew and me, but not each other. And they did not want to live together. So Daddy stayed in his house and Mommy moved out. She moved to a little house in Stoneybrook. She brought Andrew and me with her. Now Andrew and I live with Mommy most of the time, and with Daddy every other weekend, and on some vacations and holidays.

Guess what. Mommy and Daddy are married again, but not to each other. Mommy married Seth Engle. He is my stepfather. Daddy married Elizabeth Thomas. She is my stepmother. And that is how Andrew and I got two families.

This is my little-house family: Mommy, Seth, Andrew, me, Rocky, Midgie, and Emily Junior. Rocky and Midgie are Seth's cat and dog. Emily Junior is my rat. (I named her after Emily Michelle.)

This is my big-house family: Daddy, Elizabeth, Nannie, Emily, David Michael, Kristy, Sam, Charlie, Andrew, me, Shannon, Boo-Boo, Crystal Light the Second, and Goldfishie. Nannie is Elizabeth's mother, which makes her my stepgrandmother. Nannie came to the big house after Daddy and Elizabeth adopted Emily. (Emily was born in a faraway country called Vietnam.) They needed somebody to help take care of her. David Michael, Kristy, Sam, and Charlie are Elizabeth's kids, so they are my stepbrothers and stepsister. David Michael is seven like me. (Well, he is a few months older.) Sam and Charlie go to high school. And Kristy is thirteen. I adore Kristy. She is one of my most favorite people ever. And she is a baby-sitter. She baby-sits for David Michael and Emily and Andrew and me all the time. I am gigundoly glad to have a big sister.

The other people at Daddy's house are actually pets. Not humans. Shannon is David Michael's puppy. Boo-Boo is Daddy's old tiger cat. And Crystal Light the Second and Goldfishie are fish. They belong to Andrew and me.

Now you know why my brother and I are Andrew Two-Two and Karen Two-Two. (By the way, I got that name from the title of a book Ms. Colman read to our class. It is called *Jacob Two-Two Meets the Hooded Fang*.) Andrew and I have two families. We have two houses, two mommies, two daddies, two cats, and two dogs. Plus, I have two bicycles, one at each house. I have two stuffed cats that look exactly the same. Moosie stays at the big house, Goosie stays at the little house. I have toys and books and clothes at each house. Andrew, too. This is good because we do not have to pack much when we go back and forth between Mommy's and Daddy's. I even have two best friends. Nancy Dawes lives next door to Mommy. Hannie Papadakis lives across the street from Daddy and one house down. Nancy and Hannie are in Ms. Colman's class, too. We call ourselves the Three Musketeers.

Sometimes I do not like being a two-two, but mostly it is okay. Andrew and I usually get to celebrate holidays two times, once with each family. And maybe — maybe — we would be able to go trick-or-treating two times this year. Even if we did not, I wouldn't care. I could still look forward to the Halloween parade, the contests, the party, and the haunted house.

"Hurry up, Halloween!" I whispered.

3

Karen's Pumpkin Patch

"May I have your attention, please?" said Daddy.

I looked up from my lunch. Emily and my brothers and I had finished playing with the costumes in the trunk. We had put everything away. Then Kristy had called us to the kitchen.

Now I was sitting at the table with my big-house family. We were eating soup and sandwiches. And Daddy was going to make an announcement. (Ms. Colman is always making Surprising Announcements at school. Surprising Announcements are usually fun.)

"The yard," said Daddy, "needs some work. It is messy and overgrown."

"Except for the grass," interrupted Charlie. "I cut the grass last weekend."

"Except for the grass," agreed Daddy. "So I would like everyone to help out in the yard this afternoon. I will give each of you a job."

Boo. This was not a fun announcement at all. I wanted to go over to Hannie's house instead. We had planned to make clothes for my rat.

"Emily and Andrew," said Daddy, "you will help Nannie weed the garden in the front yard. David Michael, you will help your mom in the herb garden. Kristy, you will trim the grass by the driveway. Sam and Charlie, you will clean the gutters. And Karen, you will help me in the vegetable garden."

I happen to like vegetable gardens. I like them very much. Once, in the summer, I took a plane trip all by myself to visit Seth's parents in the state of Nebraska. They live on a farm. And I helped to grow vegetables. I picked them, too. That was the best part. But today I did not feel like gardening. Emily Junior needed a new outfit.

"Daddy?" I said.

"Yes, Karen?"

"Do I *have* to work in the vegetable garden?"

"Everybody is going to work in the yard today," he answered. "If you do not want to work in the vegetable garden, you may work somewhere else."

I scrunched up my face. "That's okay. I will help you." I sighed loudly.

"Thank you," said Daddy.

When lunch was over Daddy and I walked through the backyard. The vegetable garden is in a corner. (Luckily, it is *not* right next to the witch's backyard.)

"Okay. What do I have to do?" I asked. I was pouting.

"Before you do anything," Daddy replied, "I want you to see something."

He led me through the rows of eggplants and tomato plants and beans and carrots and turnips and potatoes. Not much was left. The vegetable garden was getting ready for autumn and winter.

I guess I had not been in the garden for a very long time, because I did not even know that in the spring Daddy had planted . . .

"Pumpkins!" I cried. "A whole pumpkin patch!"

Behind the other vegetables were dozens and dozens of bright orange pumpkins. Big ones, little ones, fat ones, skinny ones, lumpy ones. The vines trailed everywhere — and everywhere I looked, pumpkins peeked back at me.

"They will be ready in time for Halloween," Daddy told me. "If we leave them on the vines until then, they will just keep on growing."

I nodded. I had spotted a huge, beautiful,

15

perfect pumpkin near the center of the patch. I remembered the Halloween party.

"Daddy?" I said. I ran to the pumpkin. "Could I enter this in the pumpkin contest on Halloween? Could this pumpkin be *mine*?"

"I will make you a deal," Daddy replied. "The entire patch can be yours if you will take care of it."

"Really? I promise to water it and to learn about pumpkins. I will even take care of them during the week. I could ride to the big house after school with Hannie."

"Okay," said Daddy. "Then the pumpkin patch is yours."

The Biggest Pumpkin Ever

A pumpkin patch was a big responsibility. I was going to be the mother to about a hundred baby pumpkins. I had to do a good job.

Andrew and I went back to the little house on Sunday night. "Seth?" I said. "I am a mother now. I need to find out about raising pumpkins. Do you know anything about pumpkins?"

"Not much," Seth answered. "Why don't you read about them?"

Mommy took me to the library after school on Monday.

"I need to find out about pumpkins," I said to the librarian.

The librarian helped me look up "pumpkins" in the card catalogue. Then she said, "We have some gardening books, too. And of course the encyclopedia. You could read about pumpkins in the encyclopedia."

That was a good idea. I looked in the encyclopedia first. I already knew some of what I found there. I knew that pumpkins are orange or yellowish. I knew you can eat the pulp. (The pulp is a pumpkin's insides.) And I knew people use the pulp in pies and puddings. Also that people carve jack-o'-lanterns from pumpkins at Halloween.

Then I read some things I did not know. I found out that some people make pumpkin *soup*. I found out that most pumpkins weigh nine to eighteen pounds . . . and that big kinds of pumpkins can weigh sixty-five pounds or more.

"Sixty-five pounds!" I exclaimed.

"Shhh!" hissed Mommy. "Indoor voice, Karen. You are in a library."

"Sorry," I whispered. "But sixty-five pounds is a lot. That is more than *I* weigh. I wonder if my beautiful pumpkin is the large kind. I wonder if he could grow to sixty-five pounds. I better see what I can find out in these other books."

That day the librarian showed me two very wonderful books. One was called *The All-Around Pumpkin Book*, by Margery Cuyler. The other was called *The Biggest Pumpkin Ever*, by Steven Kroll. I especially liked Mr. Kroll's book. It is about two mice growing a big, beautiful pumpkin for a contest. Just like me! I checked both books out of the library.

On Tuesday I rode home from school with Hannie. She came with me to my pumpkin patch at the big house. She helped me water the pumpkins.

"This pumpkin," I said, showing Hannie the extra-special one, "is the pumpkin I am

going to enter in the contest. I think he will win *two* prizes — most beautiful, and biggest. Maybe he will even be the biggest pumpkin the judges have ever seen in their whole lives."

"I am going to enter one of the contests, too," Hannie told me.

"You are?"

"Yes. A jack-o'-lantern contest. I have been drawing scary faces. I want to practice a lot before I draw a face on my Halloween pumpkin."

Hannie and I talked about the contest while we worked in the garden.

"There is so much to do," I told Hannie later. "Every time I am in the patch I have to remember to turn my pumpkin a little. I do not want him to get a soft spot by lying in one position too long. And I have to fertilize my pumpkin. Guess what else I am going to do for him."

"What?" said Hannie.

"Feed him sugar water. That is what the mice do in *The Biggest Pumpkin Ever*. And their pumpkin wins first prize and gets a blue ribbon."

"Gosh," said Hannie.

"I hope there's enough time for my pumpkin to grow to sixty-five pounds," I added. "I am not sure there is. But I will let him grow until Halloween, until the very day of the contest. I will not cut him from the vine until then."

5

King Kong

"The pumpkin ran away," I sang softly. "Before Thanksgiving Day."

"Karen, why are you thinking about Thanksgiving?" Ricky Torres asked me. "It is not November yet. It is not even October."

"I am not thinking about Thanksgiving. I am thinking about pumpkins," I replied. "Big, fat pumpkins."

Ricky Torres is in Ms. Colman's class with Hannie and Nancy and me. He sits next to me in the first row. We have to sit up front because we are glasses-wearers. Ricky is my pretend husband. We got married on the playground one day.

"Well," said Ricky, "why are you thinking about pumpkins, then?"

"Because of my pumpkin patch."

Ricky narrowed his eyes. "You have a pumpkin patch?" he asked.

"Yup," I replied. Then I added, "Honest." (Sometimes the kids in my class do not know whether to believe me. They say I brag.)

"She really does have a pumpkin patch," said Hannie. "I have seen it myself."

A bunch of kids were gathering around me.

"A whole *patch*?" asked Natalie Springer.

"A whole patch. Daddy planted it in the spring when he planted our vegetable garden. Only I did not know it. When he showed it to me last week it was *full* of pumpkins. And I am in charge of them. I am the mother of those pumpkins. One of them is just gigundo," I went on. "Daddy said I could have him if I would take care of the patch. I am going to enter him in the pumpkin contest on Halloween. He will win most beautiful pumpkin. I am sure of it. Maybe he will win biggest pumpkin, too."

"He?" said Bobby Gianelli.

"Yes," I replied. "My huge pumpkin is named King Kong, because he is so big. I call him Kong for short. Kong is his nickname."

"Boy," said Pamela Harding. "I have not even started looking for a Halloween pumpkin. And you have already picked yours out, Karen."

"Hey, Karen, what are you going to do with the rest of the pumpkins?" asked Ricky. "I never knew anyone with a whole patch."

Hmm. That was a good question. What *was* I going to do with all those pumpkins? Nannie could use a few of them for pies and soup, but an awful lot would be left over. Then I thought of something. I had

Halloween pumpkins, and soon my friends would *need* Halloween pumpkins.

"Everybody," I said, "how would you like to buy your pumpkins from me this year? I will give you a good deal."

"Buy them from you?" repeated Natalie.

"Yup. You could come to my yard and pick them out of the patch."

"Cool," said Natalie.

"Awesome," said Ricky and Bobby.

Pamela just said, "I will have to think about it." That is because Pamela and I do not get along very well. But I knew she would come to her senses by Halloween. She would buy her pumpkin out of my patch just like everyone else.

Then Hannie pulled me into a corner of the classroom. "Karen," she whispered, "I have an idea. Could I pick out my pumpkin ahead of time? The one I will carve for the contest? Then I could visit the patch and watch my pumpkin grow. That would be so, so special."

"Sure!" I replied. "Whenever you want."

"Okay," replied Hannie. "Thanks!"

All that day, I thought about my pumpkin patch. And about Kong, my great, big, beautiful pumpkin.

6

Mischief Night

"Milk," I said to David Michael. I handed him the carton.

"Milk," he repeated. He put the milk in the refrigerator.

"Kleenex," I said.

"Kleenex." David Michael set it on the kitchen counter.

"Cat food."

"Cat food."

"Toilet paper."

"Toilet — hey!" David Michael lowered

his voice. "Does this remind you of anything?" he whispered to me.

"The toilet paper? No," I replied.

"Okay. I will tell you later."

I was at the big house one day after school. Elizabeth had just come home from work with five bags of groceries. She gave David Michael and me the job of putting them away.

"Tell me now," I begged.

"Shh! No. Later," replied my brother.

As soon as we were finished with the groceries, I pulled David Michael into the den. "Now tell me," I said.

"Mischief Night." David Michael grinned at me. "Get it?"

I grinned back. "Oh, yeah. Mischief Night . . . toilet paper . . ."

"Soap and shaving cream," added David Michael. "We better start stocking up on things. We want to be prepared."

I do not know if the kids in your town do anything special on the night before Halloween. But in Stoneybrook we do. We call that night Mischief Night. It is the time when kids run around after dark and make mischief. They decorate people's trees and bushes with toilet paper. They scribble on their windows or their cars with soap. They spray a little shaving cream around. Mischief-makers have to be very careful, because they do not want anyone to catch them. If people saw them making mischief, they might not give them candy on Halloween.

I had never been out on Mischief Night myself.

"Do you think we are old enough to go out this year?" I asked.

"Sure," said David Michael. "I bet our friends will be going out. I bet Hannie and Linny and Bill and Melody will be going out." (Linny is Hannie's older brother. Bill and Melody Korman live two houses away from Hannie. Melody is my friend and Bill is David Michael's.)

"Really?" I said.

"Let's call them and find out."

So David Michael phoned them and they *were* going to make mischief.

"Come on. Now let's tell my mom and your dad," said David Michael.

Elizabeth and Daddy did not like the idea one bit.

"I am sorry. You may *not* go out on Mischief Night," said Daddy.

"Absolutely not," agreed Elizabeth.

"Boo," I replied. But I knew better than to argue.

The next day, David Michael and I talked about Mischief Night again. We remembered to whisper in case any adults were around.

"I am still going to save toilet paper," announced my brother.

"What's the point?" I asked.

He shrugged. "You never know. Anyway, maybe we cannot make mischief on Mischief Night, but I bet our parents will let us protect our yard. *Other* kids will be out. We have to defend ourselves. Boy, I hope the big kids do not do anything too awful. You know what? I think they have already been smashing pumpkins."

Smashing pumpkins? Uh-oh.

7

King Kong's Cage

"Are you sure that pumpkins are already being smashed?" I asked David Michael. I had to be certain about this. It was important.

"Well, I saw one smashed pumpkin," he replied.

"Where do you think it came from?"

"Someone's front porch, I guess. It had not been scooped out and carved. There were seeds all over the street."

Oh. Off of someone's front *porch*. A pumpkin sitting right out where everyone could see it. That was a mistake. Kong was safe, though, I decided. You could not see the pumpkin patch from the street. Hardly anyone even knew I *had* a pumpkin patch. Except for the people in my two families. And except for Hannie and Nancy. And except for everybody else in Ms. Colman's class.

I wondered if I should cut Kong from his vine and keep him in Daddy's house until Halloween. But if I did that, he would stop growing. He might win a prize for the most beautiful pumpkin. But he probably would not win the blue ribbon for biggest pumpkin in Stoneybrook. And I would never know if he could have grown to sixty-five pounds . . . or maybe even bigger. I had looked up pumpkins in the *Guinness Book of World Records*. Guess how much the world's largest pumpkin weighed. Six-*hundred*-and-seventy-one pounds. How would I know if Kong could be a record-breaking pumpkin if I cut him from his vine now? I wouldn't. So I would have to leave

Kong in the patch. That was that.

In fact, I planned to leave him on the vine right up until my big-house family piled into our van on Halloween to ride downtown for the contests and the parade and the party. I wanted to give him the best chance I could.

But maybe I should protect Kong, I thought. Just in case some mean person finds out about him. It was up to me to make his patch safe.

"Charlie?" I said. "Could you please help me with something?"

"Sure," he answered. "What is it?"

"I need a cage for King Kong."

"Excuse me?"

"I want to put a fence around the pumpkin patch."

"Oh," said Charlie. "That's a good idea."

"Can we do it now?"

"We can if that roll of chicken wire is still in the garage. We will need chicken wire and some wooden stakes and some nails and a hammer."

Charlie and I looked in the garage and the toolshed. We found everything. "Let's get to work!" I said.

Guess what. Building a fence is not easy, even a little one. Charlie and I worked for two whole hours. This is what we had to do. First we pounded the stakes into the ground. We pounded in twelve of them. We put them around the edge of the patch. Then we unrolled the chicken wire. We nailed it to each stake. When we were finished, the patch was fenced in.

Charlie stepped back to look at our work. "Hmm," he said. "Something is wrong." He rubbed his chin with his hand.

While Charlie stood there thinking, Boo-Boo crept across the yard toward the pumpkin patch. Then he began to run. He leaped over the fence and landed almost on top of Kong.

"Boo-Boo!" I shrieked.

And Charlie said, "I know what is wrong! No door!"

"It doesn't matter," I replied grumpily.

"Anyone could climb right over this fence. It cannot even keep a cat out."

"Thanks a lot," said Charlie. He walked away, muttering.

Kong was not safe at all. I would have to think of something else.

8

A Home for
Every Pumpkin

Charlie did not come back to the patch.
I think he was cross with me. Well, I could
not help it. The chicken-wire fence was no
good at all.

I stepped over the fence. I sat on the
ground next to Kong. I patted his stem. "Do
not worry," I said. "I will save you, Kong.
I will think of something. The pumpkin-
smashers will not get you. You can grow
to eight hundred pounds, if you want."

"Hey, Karen, what is this?"

Hannie was standing at the edge of the

pumpkin patch. Her hand was resting on a fence post.

"It is King Kong's cage," I told her, "only it does not work. It does not even keep Boo-Boo out. I need to protect Kong from pumpkin-smashers."

"I will help you think of something," said Hannie. She stepped into the patch and sat down next to Kong and me.

Hannie and I put our chins in our hands. We thought and thought. After awhile, Hannie said, "Karen? What happens to pumpkins if you never cut them off the vine? Do they grow forever?"

"No. I don't think so. The cold weather would kill them. They would rot during the winter."

Hannie looked alarmed. "Yipes!" she exclaimed. "Karen, you better find a home for every one of these pumpkins! You do not want them to rot, do you? That would be very sad."

"You're right!" I said. "I cannot leave these pumpkins here to die." I looked around the patch. "But, Hannie, there are so *many* pumpkins. I will have to find lots and lots of homes. That will be a big job."

"Well, you could start by giving a pumpkin to each person in your two families," replied Hannie.

"And you should choose your pumpkin for the contest," I added.

"Okay." Hannie stood up. She walked around the sides of the patch. Then she walked through the patch. She was careful not to step on any pumpkins. (But I sat with my arms around Kong, just in case.)

After a long, long time, Hannie said, "I choose this pumpkin." She was standing beside a perfectly round one.

"Okay, do not move," I told her. "I will be right back." I ran into the big house. I found paper and scissors and string and a marker. When I returned to the patch I made a tag. I wrote HANNIE on it with the marker. I tied it to the stem of the pumpkin.

"Thank you," said Hannie.

"You're welcome. Now I will choose

pumpkins for my families." I made tags that read: MOMMY, DADDY, SETH, ELIZ., ANDREW, D.M., E.M., KRISTY, SAM, CHARLIE, and NANNIE. I walked around the patch like Hannie had done. I tied each tag to one pumpkin. "There," I said when I was finished.

"Now twelve more pumpkins have homes," said Hannie.

But dozens and dozens of pumpkins still had no homes. Uh-oh.

"The kids in our class are going to buy pumpkins," Hannie reminded me.

"That will help a little," I said.

I tagged pumpkins for Rocky, Midgie, Emily Junior, Boo-Boo, Shannon, Goldfishie, and Crystal Light the Second. That helped a little more. But not nearly enough.

Now I had two pumpkin problems. I had to find a way to protect Kong, and I had to find homes for all the rest of those poor, stray pumpkins.

"At least *you* will have a good home," I told Kong. I gave him a hug.

"And so will Martha," said Hannie. "Kong, this is my pumpkin, Martha. I hope you two will be friends."

Hannie and I sat in the pumpkin patch with Kong and Martha for a long time that afternoon.

9

Pumpkins for Sale

One day Hannie had a gigundoly good idea. "Karen," she said, "I know how you can find homes for all those stray pumpkins."

"You do? How?" I asked.

"Have a pumpkin sale. You are going to sell pumpkins to the kids in our class anyway. Why don't you sell them to other people, too?"

"Oh, Hannie! That is awesome! A pumpkin sale. Now let me think. . . ."

* * *

This is what I decided.

I could sell my pumpkins after school and on weekends. That meant I would have to spend extra time at the big house, though. And *that* meant I would have to check out my plans with Mommy and Daddy and Seth and Elizabeth.

"Mommy," I said, "Seth. Those poor pumpkins need good homes. I just cannot let them rot in the patch." I said the same thing to Daddy and Elizabeth. My two mommies and two daddies agreed that I could sell pumpkins at the big house.

Next I decided to sell my pumpkins right out of the patch. "Won't that be fun?" I said to Hannie. "People can come into the patch and walk around and see the pumpkins growing on the vines. That is much more interesting than looking at rows and rows of pumpkins at some boring old stand. People can do that anywhere."

Then I decided that my friends in Ms.

Colman's room should have the first pick of the pumpkins. After all, I had told them a long time ago that they could buy their Halloween pumpkins from me. I would hold a private sale for my friends. They could come to the patch the day before I let anyone else come. They would be my special customers.

Finally I realized that I would have to advertise my sale. How would anyone ever know that they could go to a pumpkin patch in my backyard? So I made a big sign. It said:

PUMPKINS FOR SALE! COME TO KING KONG'S PUMPKIN PATCH!

I could put the sign up in front of the big house whenever I was there selling pumpkins. Maybe David Michael would help me. Maybe he would stand next to the sign and shout, "This way! This way to the pump-kins!" And then hundreds of people would go to my sale and adopt all the stray pumpkins.

I was doing a very good deed.

10

Hiding King Kong

Guess what. After all my great ideas, I had a horrible one. *After* my parents said I could have the pumpkin sale, and *after* I decided to hold the sale right in the patch, and *after* I made my sign, and *after* David Michael agreed to help me, I thought: Uh-oh. All those pumpkin-buyers will see King Kong. They will know where he is. Kong will be in more danger than ever.

One afternoon when I had finished watering the patch, I sat down next to

Kong. (I sat on the watering can so I would not get muddy.)

"Kong," I said, "I do not want you to worry. Soon a lot of people will be walking around the patch. But they will not pay any attention to you. I am going to put something else here, something they will pay attention to *instead*. Then I am going to disguise you. So never fear, Kong dear."

What I put in the patch was a scarecrow.

I never knew how hard making a scarecrow would be. I wanted my scarecrow to look just like the one in *The Wizard of Oz*. But we did not have any straw.

"Daddy, can we please go to a farm and get some?" I asked.

"Honey, you do not have to stuff your scarecrow with straw," he replied.

"I do if I want it to look like Dorothy's friend."

Daddy sighed. "How about stuffing him with rags?"

"No. Straw."

"I am not driving you to a farm, Karen."

"Maybe Granny and Grandad could mail me some straw." (Granny and Grandad are my grandparents who live on the farm in the state of Nebraska.)

"Karen."

"Okay, okay, okay. I will use rags."

In our garage I found an old shirt that Daddy wears when he is painting. Then I found a pair of snow pants that Emily had outgrown.

"Good start," I said. "Pants and a shirt for the scarecrow."

I made my scarecrow's head out of a balloon. Kristy lent me one of her baseball caps to put on top of the balloon. Then I stuffed the shirt and pants with rags, and glued the balloon to the neck of the shirt.

When the scarecrow was finished, I set him up in the garden. I called David Michael to come take a look at him.

"Hmm," said David Michael. "I hope he really does keep crows away."

"Why?" I asked.

"Because if a crow lands on your scare-

crow, his balloon head will explode."

"Very funny."

David Michael left the garden. I turned to Kong. "Now for your disguise," I said. "I have planned it well. Just hold still, please."

I placed a cardboard box over my pumpkin. Then I used a package of markers to color two doors and six windows. I cut a hole in the top of the box so Kong's stem could poke through. "Perfect," I said. "Your stem is the chimney. You look just like a house, Kong. No one will know you are here."

But later I showed Kong's disguise to Hannie. Guess what Hannie said. She said, "Won't people wonder why a house is sitting in your pumpkin patch?"

Uh-oh. Hannie was right.

I thought for a moment. "If anyone asks, I will tell them that it is a home for my pet garden snake. Then no one will even go near the box."

"Good idea," said Hannie. She walked

around Kong. She peered down at her own pumpkin. "How are you doing, Martha?" she asked. "You look nice and fat and healthy. Karen is taking good care of you." She paused. "Hey, Karen, you should name the scarecrow," she added.

"I already have. His name is Irv."

11

The Great Pumpkin

One morning I woke up at the big house. Autumn was in the air. My window was open, and my room felt chilly. I breathed in. I could smell damp leaves and chimney smoke. Someone had built a fire.

I climbed out of bed and crept to the window. I looked outside. I hoped I could see smoke coming from the chimney. Then I would know who was lucky enough to have a fire in their fireplace.

But I did not see smoke curling into the air. Instead I saw something orange and horrible in the street. It was . . . a smashed pumpkin.

"Yikes!" I cried. "Kong!"

I did not even bother to change out of my nightgown. I threw a sweat shirt on over it. I scrambled into a pair of boots. Then I ran all the way downstairs and outside. The air was freezing and the ground was stiff with frost, but I kept running. I did not stop until I was in the pumpkin patch, standing by Kong's house. I saw his stem poking through the chimney hole. Then I knew he was safe.

"That was scary, Kong," I told him. "I guess your house is a good disguise, though." I lifted up the house and set it aside. Kong needed sunshine during the day. I would put the house back at nighttime.

After breakfast, David Michael and Andrew and Emily and I looked at the smashed pumpkin in the street. Seeds were everywhere.

"Poor, poor pumpkin," I said.

"Pumpkin," repeated Emily.

"Pumpkin-smashers are meanie-mos," said Andrew.

"Meanie-mos," repeated Emily.

"This is a tragedy," said David Michael. (Emily Michelle could not say tragedy.)

I spent a lot of the day in the pumpkin patch with Kong and Irv and Martha. The longer I stayed there, the warmer the day became. It felt like spring. But I knew it was Indian summer.

"Daddy?" I said sometime during the afternoon. "May I sleep in the pumpkin patch with Kong tonight? I have to protect him."

"Oh, honey, I don't know."

"But the pumpkin-smashers have been making trouble. And anyway now it is warm because it is Indian summer. Please? Sleeping in the patch will be just like camping out. . . . Puh-*lease*?"

Finally Daddy said I could sleep in the patch. But he said he would make me come inside if it got cold. I felt like Linus, who waited for the Great Pumpkin in the Peanuts cartoon.

After dinner I went to Kong's patch. I took a sleeping bag and a flashlight with me. I asked David Michael and Andrew and Kristy if they wanted to come with me, but they all said no. I hoped I would not be bored.

I was not bored.

There were an awful lot of sounds to listen to in that patch at night. I lay in my sleeping bag and stared up at the round yellow moon. Nearby, something rustled. Yikes! What was it? I held my breath, but nothing happened. I heard another rustle. Had the pumpkin-smasher come?

Rustle, rustle.

I decided the pumpkin patch was not a comfortable place for sleeping.

" 'Bye, Kong!" I called. (Kong was snug in his house.) " 'Bye, Irv. 'Bye, Martha. See you guys tomorrow!"

I fled into the big house. Everybody was still up.

"I could not fall asleep on that bumpy ground," I told my family.

"Yeah, right," said David Michael.

"Well, I couldn't."

So I slept in my bed that night. The next morning, I checked on Kong as soon as I woke up. He was still safe.

12

The Snake Patch

Halloween was coming soon. In school we wrote scary stories and talked about our costumes. At home, Hannie worked on designs for Martha's face. I saved toilet paper (just in case). And of course I took care of Kong and my pumpkin patch. I decided it was time to start my sale.

"Private sale! Private pumpkin sale!" I announced to the kids in Ms. Colman's room. "Have first pick of the patch. Come on Wednesday before the best pumpkins are taken!"

On Wednesday afternoon I rode home with Hannie. I ran across the street to the big house. David Michael was already home from his school.

"Can you help me with the private sale?" I asked him.

"Sure!" David Michael sounded pleased to be asked.

"Stay in the patch with me this afternoon," I said. "I am going to disguise Kong in his house. Do not let anyone look under the box. Try to make people look at Irv instead."

Before long my friends began to arrive. Mrs. Springer brought over Natalie and the twins. Mrs. Dawes brought over Nancy. Mr. Reubens brought over Hank and Ricky and Bobby. Hannie walked across the street by herself.

"Hi," said Natalie. "Nice pumpkin patch. Where is Kong?"

"Kong is not for sale," I told her.

"I know, but I want to see him."

Guess what. So did everybody else.

I sighed. I glanced at David Michael. He said, "Hey, everyone, come look at Irv instead. Karen made this scarecrow by herself."

A few kids wandered over to Irv. (His head had shrunk.) But Natalie saw Kong's house. "Karen, what's that?" she asked.

"Oh, nothing. Just the house where my pet snake lives."

"Your pet snake?" Natalie backed away.

Bobby leaned over the house and looked more closely. "That box is covering a pumpkin!" he exclaimed. "I can see the pumpkin stem."

My friends gathered around the box. "I bet that is Kong!" said Hank.

"Well, don't lift it up! Karen keeps her snake in there!" shrieked Natalie. "This is not a pumpkin patch. It's a snake patch!"

"Come on, you guys. Why don't you pick out your pumpkins?" I said.

Ricky left Kong's house. He walked around the patch. "I like this pumpkin," he said. "No, this one. . . . No, this one!"

Ricky liked just about every pumpkin he saw.

While Ricky was making up his mind, Pamela and her friends Jannie and Leslie arrived. Their noses were in the air. They are Gigundo Snobs.

"These are not such great pumpkins," said Pamela. "That one is lumpy. And I think *that* one has worms."

"Karen!" called Bobby. "I found the pumpkin I want!"

"Goody!" I ran to him. "Okay. Which one?"

"That one." Bobby pointed to Kong. "I will pay you one hundred dollars for him."

"He is *still* not for sale. . . . Has *any*one found a pumpkin yet?" I asked.

"I found four," said Ricky.

"I am going to buy this teensy one," said Pamela. "Maybe it will win the prize for puniest pumpkin."

I did not care *why* Pamela bought a pumpkin, as long as she bought one. So Pamela bought the baby pumpkin. Then

Bobby chose a different pumpkin. Then Ricky bought a pumpkin for every person in his family. Natalie decided not to buy a pumpkin from a snake patch, but lots of other kids bought pumpkins. And Hannie took Martha home.

I decided my private sale had been a success.

13

The Pumpkin Zoo

The next day, David Michael and I put up the pumpkin sale sign in the yard in front of the big house. My brother said he would stay in the yard and tell people how to get to the pumpkin patch. I would stay in the patch and be the salesperson. Also, I would guard Kong.

As soon as the sign was up, someone stopped her car and called, "Where is King Kong's Pumpkin Patch?" (I had not even had time to run to the backyard.)

"It's this way," I said. "Follow me."

The woman parked her car. She and two children, a boy and a girl, climbed out. They followed me to the patch.

"Come on in and walk around," I said. "Pick your own pumpkins."

The boy and the girl leaped over the chicken-wire fence. They ran all over the place. They stepped on the vines. I waited for their mother to tell them to settle down, but she did not.

"Be careful of the pumpkin babies," I said to them.

Then some more people came into the backyard.

"Welcome to King Kong's Pumpkin Patch," I said politely. "Go right in."

Soon about eight people were walking around, looking at the pumpkins. A couple of them wanted to know about Kong's house. When I told them it was the home of my garden snake they moved away fast.

"Hi, Karen!" someone called. Sam was walking across the yard to the patch. "Need any help?" he asked.

I looked at my customers. "Maybe," I replied. "Can you make sure people do not step on the pumpkins?"

"Sure." Sam stood in the middle of the patch. He told people he was from the Pumpkin Police. Everyone listened to him.

It pays to be tall.

Finally a young man said to me, "Miss? I have found a pumpkin."

"Oh, good. Which one?"

"That one." He showed me a medium-sized pumpkin near the edge of the patch. "It is a beauty," he added.

Well, that was nice, but I realized I did not know a thing about this man who wanted to leave with one of my pumpkins. I had to make sure the pumpkin was going to a good home.

Once, a stray cat gave birth to a litter of kittens in our toolshed. Daddy said I could find homes for the kittens. That was an important job. I knew I could not give the kittens to just anybody. I had to find the right home for each kitten.

I figured it was the same with my pumpkins.

"Do you like pumpkins, sir?" I asked the man.

"Well, yes."

"What do you do for a living?"

"A living? I repair cars."

"And where will you be keeping this pumpkin?"

"Karen, what are you doing?" asked Sam.

He was standing behind me. I guess he had been listening.

"I have to make sure this guy is going to give the pumpkin a good home," I whispered to Sam.

"For heaven's sake," said Sam. "The point is to sell the pumpkins. If you do not get rid of them, they will rot."

I pouted. "Okay, then I will *keep* the pumpkins. I will put them in my room. I will start a pumpkin zoo."

"Karen!"

"Sam, I cannot do this. I cannot sell my

pumpkins to complete strangers."

In the end, I had to go inside. Sam sold the pumpkins for me. In return, I gave him some of the money. I gave David Michael some of the money, too. Boo. At least Kong was still safe in his house.

14

Jack-o'-lanterns

When Mischief Night arrived, I closed my pumpkin patch. The town Halloween party was going to be held the next day. I figured nobody would want to buy any more pumpkins. It was too late.

Sam and David Michael had sold an awful lot of pumpkins for me. Only a few were left in the patch. I decided to leave them on the vines for awhile. I would figure out what to do with them later. Maybe we could use them for pumpkin pie or pumpkin soup.

Not even the pumpkins for the people in my families were left in the patch. We had already brought them inside. But Kong was still in the patch and still growing. I did not think he weighed six-hundred-and-seventy-one pounds. But he sure was big. He was one of the biggest pumpkins I had ever seen. He was enormous. He deserved his name.

On Friday, Mischief Night, Mommy drove Andrew and me to the big house earlier than usual. We wanted to carve our pumpkins in the afternoon. That way, they could glow in the windows at night.

Daddy and Elizabeth were still at work. But everybody else gathered for pumpkin carving. Even Sam and Charlie.

"Jack-o'-lantern time!" said Nannie.

Nannie had spread newspapers on the table in the kitchen. Our pumpkins were lined up along the middle of the table. First we designed the faces we were going to carve. We practiced on paper. Then we drew the faces right on the pump-kins.

Emily's face was a scribble, like this:

"How is she going to carve *that*?" asked Andrew. "She cannot carve a scribble. It is impossible."

"Shh, honey," said Nannie. "I will help her."

I was carving a pumpkin I had found in the patch during the sale. I could not carve up Kong, of course. But I did not want to miss out on jack-o'-lanterns. I drew a cross face on my pumpkin.

Everybody drew a different face.

"Hannie is carving her pumpkin today, too," I announced. "Her pumpkin, Martha. She is entering Martha in the jack-o'-lantern contest tomorrow."

"What kind of face is she going to carve?" asked Kristy.

"A scary one, I think. We will find out tonight. Hannie is working on her pumpkin now. Then she will put Martha in her front window."

"Look," said David Michael. "It is almost dark out."

When our pumpkins were finished, Nannie helped us put a candle in each one. We set our pumpkins in the windows in the living room. Sam lit the candles. I turned out the light. The room was dark except for the orange glow of our jack-o'-lanterns.

"Let's look at them from outside!" I cried.

So we did. We saw a row of flickering faces.

"That is creepy," said Andrew.

My family went back inside. Do you know what David Michael said then? He said, "Nannie, *please* can Karen and I go out tonight and make mischief? Please? Linny and Hannie are allowed to go. So are Bill and Melody Korman."

"Please, please, puh-*lease*?" I added.

"Wait until your parents get home."

When Daddy and Elizabeth came back from work, David Michael and I told them we were the only seven-year-olds in the whole neighborhood who were not allowed to go out on Mischief Night. So they changed their minds.

"You may go," said Daddy, "but only for half an hour."

"And stay with your friends," added Elizabeth.

"And take flashlights," said Nannie.

"Thank you!" David Michael and I cried.

Then David Michael stuck a bag in the bushes by the front door. We filled it secretly. We put in soap, shaving cream, two eggs, and the toilet paper.

It was our secret stash.

15

Making Mischief

"Is it time? Is it time to go yet?" I asked. I was bouncing up and down in my place at the supper table.

"Karen, *please* settle down," said Daddy for about the one hundredth time.

"But, Daddy, it's Mischief Night!"

David Michael was bouncing up and down, too.

"All right. Go ahead," said Daddy.

David Michael and I put on our jackets. We ran for the front door just as the bell rang. "They're here!" I cried.

Hannie, Linny, Bill, and Melody were waiting outside. David Michael closed the door softly behind us. "We hid our stuff in the bushes," he whispered loudly. "Here is our secret stash." He found the bag.

I grabbed Hannie's hand. "Ooh, this is so exciting!" I squeaked.

"Yeah! Our first Mischief Night."

"What should we do?" I asked my friends.

For a moment we just stared at each other. Then Linny said, "Toilet paper. We will throw some toilet paper around."

"And let's make noise!" I added. "Tonight is a good time to make noise. We can yell around in the darkness."

"I am not afraid of the darkness," spoke up Melody.

"Nope. Me neither," said the rest of us.

But I was glad the streetlights were on.

We ran down our lawn to the sidewalk.

"There is Martha!" exclaimed Hannie, pointing.

"Let's go look at her," I said. "I want to see her face."

We looked both ways, crossed the street, and ran to Hannie and Linny's front door. Martha was shining through a window in the hallway just next to the door.

"Oh, Martha is a . . . what is she, Hannie?"

"She's a dragon. A scary dragon."

"Cool! I'm sure she will win a prize tomorrow. I bet nobody else carved a dragon jack-o'-lantern."

David Michael was unwrapping a roll of toilet paper.

"Hey!" cried Linny. "What are you doing? You can't make mischief in *my* yard. If you do, then I will mess up *your* yard."

"Sorry," said David Michael. "Okay. Let's get going."

We yelled and hollered. We ran into the next yard. David Michael tossed some toilet paper into a tree. Bill and Melody draped some over a hedge.

"Where is the shaving cream?" I whis-

pered. "I want to squirt shaving cream."

Linny and I squirted the shaving cream onto the sidewalk. We wrote HELLO.

Then Hannie whispered to me, "Hey, where are the eggs?"

We looked in the secret stash. There were our two eggs.

The girls said the boys could throw them. They did not throw them at a window or anything. Eggs are a big mess to clean up. Instead, the boys threw them in the street. We watched them smash.

Splat, splat!

"What time is it?" I called a few minutes later.

David Michael looked at his watch under a streetlight. "Time to go home," he said.

"Oh, well. Tomorrow is Halloween," I replied. "The day of the contests."

We walked back to our houses. The neighborhood was quiet. Nobody had made any mischief in *our* yards.

"Good night!" I called to Hannie. "Kong and I will see you and Martha tomorrow!"

The Pumpkin-Smashers

When I woke up on Halloween morning, the first thing I did was look out my window. I was hoping for sunny weather. I did not know what would happen to the Halloween party if it rained. The party, the contests, and the parade were going to be held outdoors.

"Please, please be sunny," I said as I pulled aside the curtain.

I looked up at the sky. Perfectly blue!

Then I looked down at our yard.

Uh-oh.

Our yard was a gigundo mess. So was Hannie's and so was Melody's. The entire neighborhood was a gigundo mess. The big kids must have made mischief after my friends and I had gone to sleep.

This is what I saw. Daddy had climbed a ladder. He was pulling toilet paper streamers out of a tree. Charlie was hosing down the sidewalk. Kids had written on it with soap and crayon. There was a broken egg on the roof under my window. Shaving cream covered our front steps.

Suddenly Mischief Night did not seem like so much fun. I decided that next year I would stay home on Mischief Night.

Guess what I was going to wear that morning. My Halloween costume. (I was a witch again.) Hannie and I planned to walk in the parade together after the pumpkin contests. We could wear the blue ribbons we were going to win.

I ate breakfast with a Teenage Mutant Ninja Turtle (David Michael) and a teddy bear (Emily Michelle). When I finished I

said to them, "Guess what time it is now."
I tried to look very important.

"Nine-thirty," said David Michael.

"No! I mean, guess what it is time to do now." (David Michael shrugged his turtle shoulders.) "It is time to cut Kong from his vine. Then I will weigh him. I am pretty sure he does not weigh six-hundred-and-seventy-one pounds, but that is okay. He is huge and beautiful."

I left David Michael and Emily in the kitchen. I ran outside to my pumpkin. "Hello, Kong!" I called. "Happy Halloween! Today is your big — " I stopped talking. Kong's cardboard house had been turned over.

Kong was gone. I gasped. "Kong! King Kong! Where are you?"

I looked everywhere, but I did not see my pumpkin. Someone had cut him from his vine, and I thought I knew who.

I ran back to the house. "Sam!" I yelled.

"What?" Sam was in the kitchen. He was drinking milk straight out of the carton, which he is not allowed to do.

"Where is Kong?" I demanded.

"I don't know."

"Yes, you do! You took him. You are mad because you had to sell the pumpkins for me. So you took Kong as a mean joke."

"I did not!" cried Sam.

"Then Charlie did. He is still mad about that fence thing."

"Karen, Charlie did not take Kong, either."

"Someone did!" I shrieked. "Someone stole Kong!"

"Karen, what on earth is going on?" asked Daddy. He ran into the kitchen.

"Someone stole Kong! He is gone. He is not in the pumpkin patch!"

"Please quiet down," said Daddy. "Nobody in the family took Kong. We all know how much he means to you. Let's go look for him together."

"Thanks, Daddy," I said, "but you do not have to look for Kong with me. I will go by myself. I know where I have to look."

17

Good-bye, Kong

I knew that I should look for Kong in the street.

The pumpkin-smashers must have gotten to him on Mischief Night.

I went out our front door. I walked across our lawn to the sidewalk. There were no pumpkins in the street *right* in front of the big house, but I could see several further away.

The first one I came to had no seeds. It must have been a carved pumpkin. It could not be Kong.

The next pumpkin was very small. It could not be Kong, either.

I turned around and walked in the other direction. I passed the broken jack-o'-lantern. Then I came to a gigundo pumpkin mess.

I knew it was Kong.

I sat on the sidewalk and began to cry.

"Kong," I said, "how could anybody do this to you? You were the most beautiful pumpkin ever. Now you cannot be in the contest. You did not even get to see Halloween. This is so, so sad."

After awhile I went back to our house. I looked in the toolshed. I found a trowel and a plastic bucket. I took them back to Kong. Then I scooped up the biggest pieces of Kong and put them in the bucket.

I carried the bucket all the way to the pumpkin patch. I was just sitting there with it when I heard Kristy call, "Karen?"

"I'm in the patch," I told her.

Kristy sat down beside me. "What is that?" she asked. She pointed to the bucket.

"That is Kong," I told her. "He was smashed in the street."

"Are you sure it's Kong?"

"Positive. I would know him anywhere."

"Oh, Karen," said Kristy. "I am so sorry." Kristy put her arm around me and I cried some more.

"I should have brought Kong inside," I sobbed. "I know I should have. But I wanted to see how big he could get."

"It isn't your fault Kong was smashed," Kristy told me. "Kong had a right to be in his patch. Someone stole him. That was wrong."

I felt a teeny bit better. Even so I said, "Kristy? I would like to be alone now."

"Okay," replied Kristy. "I understand." Kristy left the patch.

For a long time, I just sat and stared at Kong. But soon I heard a rustling noise. I knew I was not alone anymore.

18

The Worst Halloween Ever

I could hear sniffling. Someone was crying. I did not think it was Kristy. Hey! Maybe it was the pumpkin-smasher! Maybe he (or she) had come back to say he (or she) was sorry about Kong.

"Hello?" I called.

"Karen?"

It was Hannie. I wondered why she was sniffling. Had she caught a cold?

"I'm back here," I replied. "Back where Kong used to be."

Hannie stepped into sight. "You've been

crying, Karen," she exclaimed.

"So have you. What's the matter?"

"You tell me first," said Hannie.

I sighed. "Kong is dead. The pumpkin-smashers got him last night. I found him in the street this morning. Now I cannot enter him in the contest. Unless there is a contest for smushed pumpkins."

"Oh," said Hannie. "Well, the pumpkin-smashers got Martha, too."

"What?" I cried. "But how could they? Martha was inside."

Hannie shook her head sadly. "Last night I put her out on our front porch. Someone pushed open the screen door, reached around, stole Martha, and smashed her in the street. I know it was Martha because there were no seeds."

"So that was Martha," I replied. "I saw her this morning when I was looking for Kong. But I never thought that pumpkin was Martha. I thought Martha was safe."

"I am sorry about Kong," said Hannie.

"And I am sorry about Martha." I

showed Hannie the bucket with the pieces of Kong inside. "This is all that is left of Kong," I told her.

"And this is all that is left of Martha." Hannie reached into her pocket. She pulled out a short, burned-down candle.

"This is a gigundoly sad day," I said.

"It is the worst Halloween ever," she added.

Hannie and I sat in the pumpkin patch and cried together for awhile.

Sniff, sniff, sniff.

After a few minutes, Hannie sat up straighter. "A few pumpkins are still left," she said, looking around.

"They are the ones nobody wanted," I told her.

Hannie pointed to a small pumpkin. "Maybe that one would win the prize for puniest pumpkin," she said hopefully.

I shook my head. "Darn old Pamela has the puniest pumpkin, remember?"

"Oh, yeah. Are you *sure* it is the puniest?"

"Pretty sure. And I would not want to lose the puny pumpkin prize to Pamela. That would be awful."

"Yeah." Hannie looked around some more. Then she pointed to another pumpkin. It was lumpy and long. "Hey, Karen. Do you think *that* pumpkin looks like a cat?" Hannie leaned over and held it up.

Actually, I did not think the pumpkin looked like a cat at all. It just looked like a lumpy pumpkin. But I wanted Hannie to feel better. So I said, "Well, maybe. Maybe it looks a little like a cat."

"Yeah, a little," agreed Hannie. "You know what we could do?"

"What?"

"We could enter it. I bet nobody else has a pumpkin that looks like a cat."

"Probably not. So do you want to enter it?" I asked.

"I guess so. Do you?"

"I guess so."

And that was how Hannie and I found a pumpkin for the contest.

19

The Contest

"**O**kay, load 'em up!" shouted Sam.

Sam was downstairs. All the big people at Daddy's house were downstairs. I was upstairs with the Ninja Turtle, the teddy bear, a monster (that was Andrew), and a jack-o'-lantern. Guess who the jack-o'-lantern was. Hannie. She had chosen a jack-o'-lantern Halloween costume because of Martha and the contest. Now she did not have Martha. And she could not enter the jack-o'-lantern contest.

Hannie said she was a little depressed.

"Load 'em up!" shouted Sam again. He wanted us to come downstairs. It was time to drive to the Halloween party. Sam's job was to load us kids into the van.

David Michael, Emily, and Andrew ran downstairs. Hannie and I followed more slowly. "I feel old today, don't you?" I said.

"Yeah. About ninety," agreed Hannie.

"Okay. Does everybody have everything?" asked Daddy. "Costumes? Pumpkins? And have you all been to the bathroom?"

We had all been to the bathroom, and the strange cat pumpkin was in a paper bag. Hannie was carrying it. I knew it would not win a prize, but I did not really care.

Daddy parked the van near the town square. Usually, the square looks like a park — with trees and benches and space to run around in. Today that space was filled with game booths and the haunted house and . . . tables covered with pumpkins and jack-o'-lanterns.

"Those are the pumpkins in the contests," I said to Hannie.

"I guess we should put Cat Pumpkin with them," she answered.

"Daddy? Hannie and I are going to enter our pumpkin in the contest," I said. "Then we want to look at the other pumpkins."

"Okay," said Daddy. "Meet us back at the van before the parade."

Hannie and I walked to the pumpkin tables. All around us were kids wearing costumes. We saw some grown-ups wearing costumes, too.

"Look, Hannie," I said. "There is the table for Biggest Pumpkin. That is where I would have brought Kong."

Hannie and I looked at the pumpkins. Some of them were awfully big.

"But Kong was bigger," I said. "He would have won."

"There are the jack-o'-lanterns," said Hannie, a moment later.

Hannie and I looked at pumpkins that had been carved with happy faces, mad faces, sad faces, surprised faces, witchy faces, clown faces, beauty queen faces, and animal faces.

"These are nice," said Hannie. "But Martha would have won."

"Where should we take Cat Pumpkin?" I wondered.

Hannie and I did not see a table for Pumpkins That Sort of Look Like Animals. So we took Cat Pumpkin to the Most Strangely Shaped Pumpkin table. We gave the judges our names, and left the pumpkin there.

"Well, that's that," I said to Hannie.

We went back to the van. My big-house family was there. David Michael, Andrew, and Emily were waiting for the parade to start. But before that happened, we heard an announcement over a loudspeaker.

"The winners of the pumpkin contests are . . ."

"The winners!" I cried. "They have already chosen the winners!"

"Shh, Karen," said Sam. "I cannot hear."

"The winner in the Biggest Pumpkin division is Connie Roland. The winner in the Jack-o'-lantern division is Arnold Werner. The winner in the Most Strangely Shaped Pumpkin division is . . ."

20

Happy Halloween!

" . . . Sandy Jackson."

"I knew we would not win," I muttered.

The judge announced the second prize winners. He announced the third prize winners. Then he announced the honorable mentions.

I stopped listening. "This is boring," I said.

"In the Most Strangely Shaped Pumpkin division," continued the judge, "honorable mention goes to Hannie Papadakis and Karen Brewer."

"See?" I said. "Kong would have won a prize."

"But Cat Pumpkin won, Karen!" cried Hannie. "Cat Pumpkin got an honorable mention. The judge just said our names! We did win!"

Well, for heaven's sake.

Hannie and I got to stand with the other people who won honorable mentions. The judge pinned white ribbons to our costumes.

Elizabeth snapped our picture.

Then it was time for the parade. Hannie and I and David Michael and Emily and Andrew got in line. Guess who got in line with us. Nancy.

"Goody!" I exclaimed. "Now the Three Musketeers can walk together."

So we did. Nancy was dressed like a dragon. (And she did not even know that Martha had been a dragon.) She had a dragon tail and dragon paws. She pretended she was breathing fire on everyone.

"But I am not an evil dragon," she said. "I am a friendly, fire-breathing dragon. Happy Halloween, Witch and Jack-o'-lantern!"

"Happy Halloween, Friendly Dragon!" I said.

We marched around the town square. When we marched by Hannie's parents, Mrs. Papadakis took our picture. When we marched by Nancy's parents, Mr. Dawes took our picture. When we marched by Mommy and Seth, Seth took our picture. When we marched by the rest of my big-house family, Elizabeth took our picture (again).

The only sad part of the parade was when Hannie and I had to tell Nancy about Martha and Kong.

"They are both smushed," I said. "They never even got to see Halloween. It is a terrible shame."

"A very terrible shame," agreed Nancy.

After the parade, the party started. The Three Musketeers dunked for apples. We ran relay races. We went to the midway and played games.

"I am good at the ring toss," said Nancy. She won a rubber spider.

"I am good at the penny pitch," said Hannie. She won a magic trick.

"I am good at the softball throw," I said. I won a sparkly pencil.

"Let's go to the haunted house!" said Hannie.

The haunted house was not as scary as we had thought it would be, but it was fun anyway. We went through it twice.

After that it was time to go home.

"Already?" I asked.

"You need to rest before you go trick-or-treating," said Daddy.

I had almost forgotten about trick-or-treating!

That afternoon, I went out to the pumpkin patch again. I sat on the watering can near Kong's empty house. I looked at the bucket that was holding what was left of

Kong. I saw his stem and some pieces of shell. Then I saw some pumpkin seeds. They were Kong's seeds. And they gave me a great idea. I could plant them! I could plant them in the pumpkin patch, and next year I would have a new crop of pumpkins, and they would be Kong's children. Maybe one would grow to be huge and beautiful and I could enter it in the pumpkin contest. And maybe Hannie would carve a jack-o'-lantern from one. Maybe I would even be able to grow a six-hundred-and-seventy-*two* pound pumpkin and then we would be in the *Guinness Book,* my pumpkin and I.

I stood up and ran inside. I had to talk to Daddy about starting the pumpkin patch over again.

About the Author

ANN M. MARTIN lives in New York City and loves animals, especially cats. She has two cats of her own, Mouse and Rosie.

Other books by Ann M. Martin that you might enjoy are *Stage Fright*; *Me and Katie (the Pest)*; and the books in *The Baby-sitters Club* series.

Ann likes ice cream and *I Love Lucy*. And she has her own little sister, whose name is Jane.

Little Sister

Don't miss #33

KAREN'S SECRET

Soon it was just me and Natalie. We were waiting for our mommies to come. Natalie kept pulling up her socks. When she was not pulling up her socks, she was chewing on her nails. I could tell she was upset.

"What's wrong?" I asked.

"Nothing," replied Natalie.

"Are you sure? You do not look very happy," I said.

"It's a secret," said Natalie.

"You can tell *me* your secret!" I said. I tried not to sound too excited. But it was hard. Secrets are neat.

LITTLE APPLE®

BABYSITTERS
Little Sister™

by Ann M. Martin,
author of The Baby-sitters Club®

More Titles... ➡

Available wherever you buy books, or use this order form.

- -

Scholastic Inc., P.O. Box 7502, 2931 E. McCarty Street, Jefferson City, MO 65102

Please send me the books I have checked above. I am enclosing $ _____
(please add $2.00 to cover shipping and handling). Send check or money order – no
cash or C.O.Ds please.

Name _____ Birthdate _____

Address _____

City _____ State/Zip _____

Please allow four to six weeks for delivery. Offer good in U.S.A. only. Sorry, mail orders are not
available to residents to Canada. Prices subject to change.   BLS995